TALES OF EARLY POLAND

TALES OF
EARLY POLAND

by

SIGMUND H. UMINSKI

ENDURANCE PRESS
Detroit, Michigan
1968

First Edition

TALES OF EARLY POLAND

Copyright 1968 by Endurance Press

Editor: DR. JOSEPH A. WYTRWAL

Library of Congress Catalog Card Number: 67-30549

Printed in the United States of America

CONTENTS

FOREWORD

THE COLLECTION of legends in this book have crossed more than seven rivers, more than seven mountains, and they were rivers and mountains red with blood. These legends come from a far-off land, lying beyond a hundred bloody rivers, beyond a hundred equally bloody mountains.

The narratives of the early Poland of the 9th and 10th centuries in this modest collection are beautiful. And in them, as in fairy tales throughout the world, all kings are valiant, all knights gallant, all princesses lovely, all horses swift and unsurpassed, every goblet is of pure gold, every sword of steel, every heart warm and eager. Also, in them, as in all fairy tales throughout the world, good always conquers and evil suffers a well deserved punishment.

According to scientific enquirers into legends and myths, every legend, whether fantastic or improbable, has some slight foundation in real facts. In other words in every legend there is a spark of truth. In short, it is somewhat similar with legends as with old proverbs. They are not only the wisdom and property of individual nations, but in fact they represent equally the wisdom and eternal property of the whole of mankind.

The legends in this book speak almost exclusively of Gniezno and Krakow. Certain characters, appearing in these legends, belong to history, namely to the oldest period recorded in our annals, of which the first date is the year 963. Mieszko, Boleslaw the Brave, St. Adalbert, Otto III, all of these are people who actually lived and worked, about whom we know a great deal from early records, from ancient annals and chronicles. Other characters, such as Piast or Lech, descend from the era in which history seems as if she is fondling her snow-white quill, not yet dipped in the ink. She dips it in the ink-pot and sets it down on a sheet of parchment in the year 963.

Upon reading the legends in this collection, dear reader, let your heart glow with admiration for the characters in every one of the legends.

In "The Legend of Krakus and the Dragon" you will read the tale of the wise king who slew a terrible dragon. If the Polish Prince, Krakus, killed the legendary dragon, this monster must have been quite a near relation of the Sphinx, which devoured the inhabitants of a town older than Cracow, namely Teb, the capital of Beocia.

"The Legend of Wanda" is the tale of Freedom,

of that priceless gift which should be the right of each and every nation. To save the freedom of her country Princess Wanda, "who desired no German," threw herself into the waves of the Vistula, one of the bloodiest rivers in the world.

"The Legend of the Piasts" is the story of how Mieszko's ancestor, Piast the ploughman, had given shelter and hospitality to two angels. This tale is very significant and touches you to the heart because it points out one of the characteristics of the Poles— their hospitality. This hospitality is shown even by the poorest. Every stranger is greeted with an old Polish motto "Gosc w Domu—Bóg w Domu" (a Guest in the House—a God in the House) and another well known motto still observed in Polish homes and displayed to this day, saying "Czem Chata Bogata" (The richness of the house). The son of the Piast who had been the hospitable host of angels, and whose cottage had received a Prince, was made ruler of Poland. He won great glory for himself, and the boundaries of his kingdom spread far and wide.

The Legend of Mieszko will excite the reader. This first Prince of Poland to be known by a foreign name, was born blind. He recovered his sight and married Dombrowka, a Czech princess and a good Christian, in order to Christianize Poland.

The story of Emperor Otto's visit to Gniezno is

heart-warming. The emperor visits the neighbor—Poland. He finds kindness and hospitality in his host. He sees that here is a neighbor whom it would be worth while to have as a friend. The emperor takes his crown from his own head, and places it upon that of *Boleslaw* saying: "Thou shall be king." In these words the German emperor recognizes the sovereignty of Poland. Not only does he recognize *Boleslaw* as King of Poland, he also raises *Gniezno* to the dignity of archbishopric, so that the Polish clergy are no longer subject to the German clergy.

More than seven hundred years ago a guard on the top of the tower of St. Mary's Church in Cracow noticed the Tartar hordes advancing from afar, sounded the alarm and roused the sleeping town, but suddenly a Tartar arrow pierced his throat. On this he had finished the tune, which from that time onwards for over seven hundred years suddenly breaks off sharply on a note as high as the heavens.

What a lovely tale! The continuation of this tune is sung to Krakow by distant Samarkand, the seat of the great Mongol powers of Timur or Tamerlaine. In 1941, when the Polish soldiers, freed from Russian prisons, barefoot and hungry, reached Samarkand and played this song, or *Marjacki* "*Hejnal*," the dwellers in the capital of Uzbekistan were filled with joy. They listened and listened, and when the melody was suddenly broken the old people recalled a certain age-old prophecy which proclaims that when the sons of Lechistan, or in other words Poles, shall some day come to Samarkand and sing this strange song in the square, then Uzbekistan will regain its freedom.

The history of Poland, like any other country, is rich with legends. Are legends true? Certainly! For hundreds of years each generation passes to the next, the rich store of legends. Some of them are known to many people in every detail and have been told and retold.

The legends in this book are from the seven rivers, from the seven mountains. The Polish legend comes from beyond a hundred bloody rivers, from beyond a hundred bloody mountains. They depict the spirit and the soul of Poland. At times the legends appear sad, however they are always beautiful. Poland's kings appear to be valiant, her knights considered gallant, all princesses lovely, and all the horses are described as swift and unsurpassed, but the eagle which became the symbol of Poland is as white as snow, on a field as red as blood.

Sigmund H. Uminski

I. The Story of Lech and Gniezno

MANY CENTURIES AGO, there lived in the Polish lands a Duke whose name was *Lech*. It was perhaps before the time of Alexander the Great. At that time, there was no town of *Poznan,* nor *Kruszwica,* nor any large city in the land of Poland. The country was wild, with few people. Men lived together in small communities, fearing the savage Goths who invaded them from the west, and the wild Huns came from the east. These invaders brought death and desolation to Polish lands. The peaceful, agricultural Slavs by necessity became warriors because they had to defend their homes and families from destruction.

The first Duke of Poland was *Lech.* He was the first ruler who established the Dukedom on the soil of Poland, and as a result assumed the leadership of the western Slavs. *Lech* united the tribes, and during his reign, Poland developed and grew prosperous. Improved strongholds were built to resist the raids of the savage neighbors. The fields were tilled and hides were cured. With the arrival of more settled times, men grew more civilized and turned to the making of pottery, agricultural implements and furniture. The patterns and styles have changed very little, and even today utensils can be seen in use, very similar to those which were used in the time of *Lech*.

In defense of his country against invaders, *Lech* kept a strong army. It was well equipped, well trained and large. The army covered itself with glory and brought fame to *Lech*, its captain. The name of *Lech* became so famous throughout the world, that his fiefs were called *Lechici*. The Muscovites often called the Poles *Lachi*, and the Turks named Poland *Lechistan*, or the country of *Lech*. Lech's power stretched over a wide area of country that the Hungarian Lengyel is believed to come from Lech.

The Duke was an outstanding man in many ways. He was very tall and broad shouldered. His strength was astounding that he could wield a battle-axe which ordinarily took two men to lift. He was handsome, with fair hair, blue eyes and well-defined features. Not only was he fearless, he was also a wise ruler, and had a great gift for learning. He had this in common with most princes. Hunting was his favorite, and his leisure was generally devoted to this sport. Just as in battle, he led the field, in hunting he always claimed the first stroke at the bear or the boar, when the beast was brought to bay. The Duke was known for his bravery and valued courage in man or beast.

Lech also loved falconry, and raised many gos-hawks and peregrine falcons, some of which he had trained himself. Once he tried to train a young buz-zard, but the bird had died when he was almost half trained. The Duke wanted to train an eagle. Although his falconers had advised him that it was impossible, he persisted in the hope that he might capture and train a young golden eagle. He thought that it would be swifter and stronger, in the flight after its quarry, than any goshawk.

One day in the spring, the Duke with his court went hawking. A large group set forth from the castle, each one dressed in the green hunting habit which Lech had instructed should be worn by all those who joined the chase with him. The Duke led the hunting expedition, and as usual rode at the head of the caval-cade. His favorite hawk he had on his wrist, and he was closely followed by his Master of the Hunt. Lech was in a thoughtful mood, and paid little attention to the conversation around him. Without a warning, he gave his bird to the 'Master of the Hunt,' saying curtly:

"I would rather be alone."

The Duke set spurs to his horse, and galloped off. His members of the hunting group were surprised and

Lech Discovers a Nest on the Hill

troubled. No man attempted to follow the Duke, because at times he was in a strange mood, and then it was better not to approach him.

Lech directed his horse forward because he had a desire to reach a hill which he noticed in the distance. After galloping a while, he reached it, and looked around. At first he was not impressed, but soon discovered a nest, perched on a rocky crag. It was a nest of a white eagle, who sat with her young ones around her. Indeed she was a noble bird, with curved beak and powerful talons, and wings wide enough to bear her aloft in graceful flight.

This was the eagle that Lech had dreamed to possess.

"If I could capture it and have it trained," he said to himself, "this bird would make falconry a delight. It would arouse the envy of every prince in Europe."

The bird overheard the Duke and stared at him, ready to attack if he should touch her or the young ones in the nest.

Lech resolved to capture one of the young. His desire was to take it home to his castle, and train it with all the care and skill at his command. What a prize this would be, if he could obtain one of those eaglets!

The Duke jumped from his horse and climbed towards the nest. The white eagle watched him, while her young ones, surprised by the approach of a stranger, crept under her wings. *Lech* shouted and waved his arms, hoping to frighten the bird from her nest, but the eagle did not stir. The Duke came nearer, and put forth his hand. The eagle, with a swift movement, pecked at him as though in warning. *Lech* did not heed this warning. Reaching for his dagger, he held it aloft, hoping that the bird would wound herself if she approached him too near. With his other hand, he attempted to grasp one of the eaglets, but the mother-bird did not warn and charged at him. The prince and the bird were both hurt. *Lech* persisted and kept reaching for one of the eaglets. He thought he could capture the young one with ease. The struggle continued. *Lech* used his dagger more freely. The eagle had been wounded several times, and blood stained the white feathers with dark crimson splashes. The eagle defended her nest and her freedom and the liberty of her little ones.

The Duke's brave and generous heart was touched with emotion by this unyielding defense and by the noble courage. The sight of the blood which trickled down the bird's white breast made him ashamed of his desire to deprive of its freedom the offspring of so valiant a mother. He turned away, and descended the hill, deeply touched. A brave bird, who spilled her blood for her freedom and for her eaglets!

Lech sat down at the foot of the hill and looked at the scene before him. Far yonder as far as his eye could reach, stretched out the fair lands of Poland, his country that he loved with all his heart. Would he not defend her, just as the eagle had defended her little ones and the nest? And suddenly a thought came to him. Let that brave, white eagle become the symbol of Poland, let her be the token of freedom for which all those worthy of the name of Pole should shed their blood, and the eagle's blood be the symbol of bravery. Poland is immortal; so shall the White Eagle be immortal. Thus to this day, on the shield and banner of Poland, is blazoned the white eagle on a crimson field.

The hill was the favorite choice of Lech. He loved that hill where he had found the eagle's nest and which still bears his name as Lech Hill. He took his counsellors to the spot and showed it to them, saying: "Let us build our nests here, as do the eagles!" As a result a castle was built, and then a city, and it was called "Gniezno," which, in the Polish language of those days, meant "nest." In those times Gniezno became a fair city, and was the capital of Lech's Dukedom, lying on the hillside which bears his name.

The White Eagle has always been on the banners of Poland. When Poland has been attacked, her sons have defended her as bravely as the eagle who long ago shed her blood in the defense of freedom.

II. The Legend of Popiel

IN THE TOWN of *Kruszwica*, beside the lake of *Goplo*, stand the ruins of an ancient castle. There can be found only one tower which remains untouched by the hand of time. It stands alone, pointing towards the sky like an accusing finger. The tower is beautiful, made of bricks, which had been mellowed with centuries into a silvery pink. It rises gracefully from the highest point of *Kujawia's* rolling, green plain. If you go up to the top of that tower, which is called the Tower of the Mice, you will be climbing up steep, spiral stairs. When you reach the top of the tower, you will be rewarded, by the beauty of the countryside, which will greet your eyes. There, below you, will be the fair fields of Poland. Into the far, far away horizon they stretch, as far as the eye can see, the fields are beautiful in their fertility, and noble in their broad expanse.

Beneath the tower, cherry and apple trees adorn the ruins of the old castle, making it gaudy with their blossom in the spring, whereas in the summer it becomes the favorite haunt of the children of *Kruszwica*.

The town itself is small today, and unimportant, but it is neat and clean and is conscious of its famous, historic past. To the north of the town stands the parish church, built in Gothic. When you enter inside, you will see the portrait of Bishop *Marcin Gall*, who was the anonymous chronicler of the tales of Boleslaw the Wry-mouthed. He was the first who wrote of Polish history, who first related the Polish legends. We owe a great debt to the good Bishop, for thanks to his scholarly pen many facts about early Polish history have been preserved, which would otherwise have been lost.

To the south of *Kruszwica* lies the Lake of Goplo which reflects the trees that grow around it in its tranquil waters. It is a long, narrow lake, which stretches towards the south, reflecting the blue sky in its glancing waters, mirroring the last golden rays of the setting sun. When the winds ruffle its placid face, its waves become irridescent and rainbow hued. To the east and west of the lake are fertile fields which sweep away to the horizon, and sway in summer, silver and gold, as the breeze ripples, with a gentle sigh and a whisper through the ripening corn. There are orchards, over which can be seen the wooden roofs of farms and villages, like islands in a sea of pink and white blossom. There are manor houses, whose roofs are taller, and which are approached by avenues of poplars. Far away in the mist is the southern shore of Goplo. It reaches into the horizon, beyond *Inowroclaw*, *Pakosc*, and *Trzemeszno*.

Many centuries ago the country was dotted with watch-towers, from the heights of which the citizens would scan the sky-line for any sign of the approaching foe. Some of these still stood until recent years, when the last World War unleashed by the Germans destroyed the last of these age-old landmarks.

Every visitor to Poland as he stands on the Polish soil, lost in contemplation of this lovely country, is a little awed, perhaps, by the beauty around him, by the sound of music which may fall upon his ears. If his visit happens to be in the month of May, he will hear hymns sung in praise of the Most Blessed Virgin, Queen of Poland.

When one visits Poland, one must realize that he is in the very cradle of that Polish Kingdom which was built up by the strong hands of the Piast dynasty which took over the rule after the Popiels had perished. They ruled over the tribe of *Polanie* or *Polans*, who settled here and assumed the leadership of other tribes, whose princes were subordinate to them. The *Polanie* built a powerful Poland and brought about the unification of the Polish nation.

Imagine that you are standing on the summit of

the Tower of the Mice. The history of that tower is told herewith.

It happened in the ninth century. Prince *Lech* and his capital of Gniezno were just memories in the minds of men. Their story came from grandfathers who had heard from their grandfathers. There were some old people who remembered *Leszek I* and *Leszek II*. The capital of the Kingdom of Poland had been removed from Gniezno to *Kruszwica*, and there reigned the second and the last Popiel. He was the worst and the most cruel of all Polish kings and princes. Perhaps only *Waclaw*, King of Bohemia and Poland, who "wept, did penance and murdered in turn," could be compared with him, although no one could match him in cunning and deceit. It cannot be believed that Polish blood flowed in his veins, for how could such wickedness be found in a Pole?

Bishop Marcin Gall gave Popiel the Latin name of "*Choscius.*" Some chroniclers state that his name was "*Chwostek,*" which, in old Slavonic means "Little Tail." Still others think, that his name was not "*Chwost*" (Tail), but "*Chwast*" which means "Weed." In truth he was akin to the bad weeds which grew in abundance in the fields of Poland, which men were obliged to uproot. His official name was *Popiel II.*

Popiel II lived in the castle of *Kruszwica* because

he did not like the city of *Gniezno* founded by *Lech*. He was not satisfied with a dwelling made of wood, as were other Polish Kings and Princes, who lived according to the old, Slavonic customs. Their castles were crowned with wooden towers, surrounded by stout wooden palisades, and they all had a moat.

Chwast was determined to have a castle made of brick, in the German fashion. He thought that he was safer in a castle built of brick, and he also felt that he would be quite secure, even if the people should eventually revolt against him. The German artisans came and built the castle of *Kruszwica*, of brick, in the German style. The townspeople were annoyed with these strangers, who were loud, bold and quarrelsome. They drank very heavily, and swaggered around the town as if they owned the country. They were clever artisans, and they built *Popiel* such a castle as had never been seen before. The castle was beautiful with a large moat and several large towers. The interior was very luxurious as the exterior was massive.

Chwastek's wife, who was a German, was very pleased with the castle. She was very beautiful, but very wicked, even more wicked and cunning than *Popiel* himself. She was tall, slender, red-haired, with slanting, green eyes and a red and lustful mouth. Her beauty was often used for evil ends. It had been said that her name was perhaps Ortrud, or Krimhilda, or even something more outlandish than that. It is enough that she was wicked, red-haired and German.

In appearance *Popiel* was a strong contrast to his wife. He was fat, with a pink face, small eyes and loose, moist lips. He had a fleshy nose and a rather receding forehead, and his hair was sparse. The only good feature he possessed was his hands, which, strangely enough, were long, thin and white. But looking closely at them, you could see that they were mean, grasping hands, more like claws than the hands of a man.

The royal couple was pre-occupied with amusement and extravagance. They imposed high taxes on the people to pay for their entertainment and extravagance. They seized everything for themselves, and left the people destitute. The nation was ruined. The people were starving and unhappy. To seek justice from the ruler was useless. Those who approached the castle, in the hope that the ruler would welcome them, were either thrown to the dogs, or locked in a cage, unarmed, with a bear. The King and Queen watched the struggles of the wretched victims with great delight. Merchants were not only plundered, but thrown into a dungeon, where they remained until ransom should be paid for them.

Popiel was a greedy ruler for he coveted the goods of others. He seized the lands belonging to his own uncles, he stole their cattle, he burned their castles, he pillaged their estates, and brought the booty which he captured to *Kruszwica*. He had to have everything to satisfy his pleasures. His food had to be perfect, his wine had to be spiced to his taste, otherwise, he would fly into a rage. He loved foreign spices, saffron, pepper and cinnamon. He spent nights in orgies which were marked by unrestrained license. If he could find gypsies, he would carry them off to his castle, and make them do their wild dances until they fell, exhausted, on the floor of the banquet hall. When *Popiel* was drunk he would shoot arrows at his own servants, and many a person was wounded or killed for his master's pleasure. He delighted in setting fires to the villages, in destroying the property of others, in witnessing their tears and misery. This was his greatest amusement. If he could provoke tears of anger, of sorrow, of real misery, then he would be content. He was a cruel German master.

All men hated *Popiel*, deep in their hearts, and they had many good reasons for this. But what could they do? *Popiel* was securely guarded by his armed courtiers. These men, hardened like their master, rough and warlike, were called "my vikings" by the King. They did not understand kindness. Their devotion to their master was perhaps due to the good living which they enjoyed in his service, rather than

for any love which they may have had for the King.
There was always abundant and good food, and plenty
of drink and high pay. They ate, drank, wenched and
lived like lords. And they always wore chain mail on
their breasts.

On several occasions the people, driven to desper-
ation, tried to revolt. They would march on the castle,
but the castle of *Popiel* could not be conquered, nor
burned down. It was built of brick. *Chwastek* always
appeared in public dressed in his armor, holding a
battle-axe. When the prisoners were brought before
him for punishment, he would use a foul language
to reprimand them. The prisoners were ordered to be
beheaded, or bound to a long, thin board. When they
were securely bound, the board would be bent back
until it formed an arc, then suddenly released. The
force of the spring would break the victim's back and
all his bones. Men were tied to horses' tails and drag-
ged over the fields until they died, or were thrust into
a deep stinking dungeon to starve and be devoured by
the rats. The King was a terrible and cruel man, but
more terrible still was the German queen. She was
wicked beyond belief, and she taught the king his
cruel ways.

There was a time when *Popiel* even roused his
own uncles against himself. Some say that he had
twelve uncles, though others assert that there were

thirty in number. Whatever was the number, they all revolted. They gathered their armies and marched on the castle, hoping to conquer it and take *Popiel* as a prisoner. The armed courtiers of *Popiel*, standing on the tower, saw them from afar. *Chwastek* gathered his defenders together and prepared for battle. The drawbridges were raised, the fire was kindled and raised to the greatest possible to heat the oil. The provisions were hastily pillaged from the townspeople. When the attacking forces tried to storm the castle, all *Chwastek's* defenses went into action. It is impossible to tell how many men were killed in the battle. The red-haired German woman was continually pleading with *Popiel*, urging him to make peace, to promise freedom to the people and to invite his uncles to a banquet feast in the castle.

Chwastek agreed and performed a comedy. He wept, and swore that it broke his heart to see so much noble blood spilt, and so many good people killed. He promised to feed the hungry, he promised to take care of the sick and the aged, he promised to be a father to the orphans and a support to the widows. He promised everything. To his uncles he was humble and submissive. He invited them to dine with him. He would do what they wished, and he prayed that they would grace his table with their presence. They believed him and they accepted. They concluded the peace which *Chwastek* so much desired. They swore oaths to their gods, oaths which it was a great sin to break, although theirs were pagan gods, for they were not Christians in those days.

The banquet feast was prepared. Whole sheep, hogs and wild boar were roasted on the spit. Strange meats, sweets and spices were boiled in saffron, fried in butter and honey; sauces were made from currants, from the juices of herbs. Besides the meat there were birds of every type, and in great quantity: grouse, black-cock, duck, geese, all prepared in many ways. Wines were in abundance, foreign, rich wines, home-brewed mead, made by the hand of the Queen herself.

In the great banquet hall the tables were loaded with food and drinks. On the stone flagged floor, sweet aromatic herbs were burning, and the light from the torches cast shadows on the arras-covered walls. These had been made by the Queen and her ladies in their leisure hours. They were worked with many fantastic scenes and bold colors mingled with one another. They, except for the long tables and rude benches, were the sole adornment of the high, vaulted banquet-hall. All the uncles were delighted and not one of them was suspicious that all was not well. The crowd was congenial and the fare was excellent. The uncles enjoyed their food and drinks. Music played by trumpeters, gaily reflected the mood of the revellers.

Chwastek himself was in his glory and beamed with happiness. His wife, richly dressed, sparkling with jewels, was beautiful and sweet. Her red hair was braided with pearls. A circlet rested on her white brow, of green, opalescent stones, which in tight-fitting gown of white velvet revealed every curve of her beautiful body, and emphasized the feline grace of her every movement. Her little waist, too, was encircled with gems and her fingers were heavy with them. Yes, she was beautiful, but evil.

The company was merry, and they did not heed the evil glint of the Queen's eyes, nor perceived that she bit her lip impatiently from time to time. They only saw that she was beautiful, that she smiled upon them, and that she kept pushing the food and drinks on them. The Queen received many compliments. As the guests grew merrier and became more fuddled, the Queen became more gracious. A smile and a look of triumph came into her eyes, as the crowd acclaimed *Popiel* and his Queen as the best sovereign in the world. The red-haired German woman rose to her feet and said: "Dear Uncles, I desire to grant me one favor. I pray you, drink a toast with me, which I will pour into your goblets!" And she poured the rich, deep gold mead into each man's goblet. She walked slowly around the table, holding the ewer aloft, moving smoothly and gracefully, conscious of her beauty.

When all the uncles had been served, they rose as one man and drank the toast which the Queen proposed: "To eternal peace." They quaffed it at one draught, not a drop remained in the goblets.

Old *Mszczuj* was the first to feel the effects of the poison which he unknowingly drank. Seized with gnawing pain, he rose suddenly from the table crying: "Treachery!" He stumbled towards the wall where hung his battle axe, and made an attempt to seize it, but his hands groped along the wall like those of a blind man. Then, he fell heavily to the ground, dead.

Bozywoj was next to feel the poison tearing at his vitals. He drew his dagger and tried to thrust it into Chwastek's breast, but the dagger fell from his fingers and in a moment he too, was dead.

The other guests were terrified, they clutched at their hearts, they gaped at the King and Queen, hardly able to believe what had befallen them. They tried to rise, overturning the benches upon which they sat, but one by one they fell to the ground, where they lay groaning on the stone flags of the banquet hall.

And *Chwastek* stood up and shouted: "I promised you eternal peace; now you have eternal peace." And he laughed, and his German red-haired woman laughed, and their laughter echoed through the castle. They laughed as the uncles groaned and cried out, they laughed as the uncles cursed them, they laughed

Popiel, Who Was Eaten by Mice

as the uncles died, one by one, and all their knights with them. Horrible was that laughter amid death, amid the curses and groans of the dying, amid the death-rattle of so many men. Horrible was that laughter ringing through the banquet hall, which was the scene of such suffering, horrible was that laughter amid the dead, whose bodies were growing rigid. Horrible was the laughter of *Popiel* and his red-haired German wife.

The last uncle died, and the royal couple looked at each other in silent triumph. There was silence for a moment, then voices were heard, crying out in fear. The clatter of feet echoed throughout, when the others fled in haste.

As the last uncle drew his last breath, out of the Goplo lake appeared myriads of mice, which advanced straight towards the castle. The sight of them terrified the servants and the soldiers who fled in all directions at their approach. The mice, in orderly array, swept up the approaches to the castle, over the draw-bridge, through the court-yard and into the banquet hall. There, they did not halt, but made straight for the King and Queen. They were horrible, fearsome creatures, grey, wet, disgusting, with their little pink eyes glistening and their little, fat bodies jostling one another. Their whiskers seemed to bristle and it was as though their lips were curled back in a snarl to

reveal their sharp, pointed teeth. There was a nau-
seating stench emanating from them, a stench of
dampness, and of death. Still they came and the royal
couple stared at them as though transfixed. The Queen
screamed and, pulling her husband after her, they ran
to the tower which adjoined the banquet hall. They
shut the heavy oak doors behind them, thinking that
they were safe.

The sound of gnawing was heard, gentle at first
and then louder and more insistent until the oak doors
shook, and finally—a hole appeared through which a
grey body leapt. Then another, and another, and soon
hundreds had rushed through the hole made in the
door. *Popiel* and his wife rushed in terror up the spiral
stairs and shut themselves in still another room, but
the mice followed them, and ate their way through
the door like locusts. Now there were hundreds, thou-
sands, millions. The sounds of struggle could be heard
as the wretched King and Queen battled with their
attackers. *Popiel* killed hundreds of the mice, but it
was a hopeless struggle, there were more and more of
these creatures. The courtiers and soldiers huddled
together outside, listening in terror to the shrieks of
rage and despair which came from the tower. Screams
for help grew louder and more desperate, but no one
had the courage to move, no one had the courage
to enter the castle. Howls of pain, horrible to hear,

were soon succeeded by whimpering and groaning, which was even more blood-curdling. After a short time the myriads of mice streamed out of the tower, through the banquet hall, out through the court-yard, past the soldiers and courtiers who were terrified, and back to the Lake of Goplo, where they disappeared into its waters.

It was several days later that the first brave men dared to enter the castle. They did so with trepidation and very, very cautiously. When they entered the banquet hall, they found the bodies of *Popiel's* uncles untouched, as they had died. But in the tower they found only the garments and jewels of *Popiel* and his Queen. Nothing more. The mice had eaten *Popiel* and his wife. They had eaten them because they were wicked, because they harmed the people over whom they reigned, because they were treacherous, because they laughed when the uncles lay dying in agony from the poison which they had received at the hands of the red-haired Queen. They ate the King and Queen, and not a trace of their bodies remained, in the Tower of the Mice, which still stands on the soil of Poland, situated on the shores of Lake of Goplo.

The castle of *Kruszwica* stood empty. There was no King. The reign was ended, and fear left the people. The mice had eaten *Popiel* and they had eaten his wicked red-haired German Queen.

III. The Legend of Krakus and the Dragon

ON THE BANKS of the Vistula River in *Krakow*, there stands a hill now known as the *Wawel Hill*. On that hill stands today a beautiful and ancient castle, and a Cathedral in which are buried the Kings of Poland. Below, nestling, as it were, under its protecting shadow, lies the city of *Krakow*, the ancient capital of Poland. It is a beautiful city, whose stones seem to speak of ancient glory and heroic deeds.

Long, long ago there was no castle on the *Wawel Hill*, only rocks and trees. There was no city of *Krakow*, only a small settlement of wooden huts inhabited by peaceful people who tilled the land and plied their trade, and prospered.

On one side of the *Wawel Hill* was a deep, dark cave. It had a forbidding look, and its entrance was overgrown with tall, rank weeds. No man had ever dared to enter that cave, and some said that a fearsome dragon lived within it. This was disbelieved by the younger generation. The old men said that they had heard their fathers tell of a dragon who slept in the cave, and no man dared to waken it, or there would be terrific consequences for them all.

Some of the young people were determined to explore the cave despite of what the older people said. They considered the tales about the dragon as foolish talk to scare the young and the children. What harm could come to them? they argued. Dragons are very good for old men to believe in, but people who do not believe old legends and have up-to-date ideas knew that such things simply did not exist.

A band of a dozen or so youths armed with torches and flints with which to light their way into the dark recesses of the cave, set out to climb the side of the hill. They were warned by their elders, but they did not heed the warning. When they reached the entrance to the cave they halted and peeked inside, trying to identify something in the darkness. They could not see anything. It was not a pleasant place, the weeds were thick and clung about their legs, the air was heavy and foul and the whole place was eerie. Even the strong-hearted and brave quailed and the boys began to look at one another doubtfully. They were ashamed of their fears and they decided to go in. They lit their torches in silence, and one by one they walked carefully into the darkness. The cave was long and narrow and the light of the torches threw fantastic shadows on the walls of the cave. It seemed

Three Boys Discover the Dragon in the Cave

to the youths, as they advanced, that they could hear a deep and regular breathing, but they still went on.

Suddenly, a few paces in front of them, they saw a large, heaving mass. It seemed to be of a greenish color and covered with scales. The boys became frightened. How could they escape fast enough without being caught, was their main concern. They did not pause at the entrance of the cave, but ran down the hill, stumbling in their haste. But when they reached the bottom of the hill they dared to look back at the entrance of the cave. At the entrance of the cave, stretching its hideous head, showing its long, sharp teeth, and evil, flashing eyes, was the dragon. It waved its head slowly from side to side, let out its blood-curdling bellow and started to come down the hill-side.

The dragon made its way towards a herd of grazing cattle which fled in terror at its approach. The hideous creature was nimbler than the cattle and, seizing one of the unfortunate animals, it carried it back into the cave. The people were stunned and terrified. Mothers clasped their children to their breasts. Men looked for their axes, and the boys who awakened the dragon form its cave slunk away, terrified that they may be the victims of the monster.

Since that day, the people knew no peace. Daily the dragon appeared and carried off a victim. Sometimes it captured a child, sometimes a sheep, sometimes even an adult. There were many attempts to kill the dragon. Men banded together, armed with axes, waiting to give the dragon its final death blow. But no axe could penetrate the strong scales, no blow could be strong enough to harm the dragon. Many men died in a brave attempt to rid their country of this terrible monster, but in vain. In the village lived a man named Krakus, who was wise and learned. The people often came to him to ask his advice if they were sick or in trouble, and he was always ready with a remedy or good advice. He was called by some people to be a magician, because he mixed draughts for the sick, or gave them herbs. But Krakus was not a magician. He was wiser than his fellows and had made experiments of various kinds with herbs and spices. The people in the village turned to Krakus for advice. Perhaps he could find some way of destroying the dragon, or at least he might be able to put it to sleep again. Krakus listened to the villagers, stroked his chin and murmured to himself. Then he asked them to bring him a young sheep, fat and tender. When the men left his house to fetch a sheep, he turned to his many jars, and started to mix a thick yellow paste from the contents of one of them. The paste had a strong, unpleasant smell. As soon as the sheep was brought, Krakus smeared it all over the animal. He quickly carried it up the hill, advanced as far as the mouth of the cave, and threw the sheep inside.

There was silence for a few moments. Finally the dragon, roaring and bellowing, rushed out of the cave and went down the hill to the Vistula River. The sheep which the dragon devoured had been smeared with sulphur and the dragon's inside stomach was on fire, and suffered from a terrible thirst. When the dragon reached the bank of the Vistula, it drank and drank. *Krakus* and the people watched from the bank, hoping for release from their suffering and constant fear. The dragon began to swell, but still it drank and swelled some more. It continued drinking till suddenly there was a great explosion, and the dragon burst.

The people rejoiced when they heard of the death of the dragon. Impressed by the wisdom of *Krakus*, the people invited him to rule over them, and they built a stronghold on the Wawel Hill, where they could scale its slopes without fear. The country prospered under the rule of *Krakus* and a city grew up around the hill which was called *Krakow* (Cracow), in honor of *Krakus*.

When *Krakus* died, the people gave him a magnificent burial, and erected a mound over his tomb which can be seen to this day. The people brought earth with their own hands to the mound, and it has endured through the centuries since its erection, a lasting monument to the love of the people for a wise and brave Prince.

IV. The Legend of Wanda

THE WISE AND BRAVE Prince *Krakus* who ruled Poland had three children, two sons and one daughter. His eldest son was destined to be the next ruler of Poland when *Krakus* died, but he was slain by his younger brother, who coveted power for himself. The people were angered by such wickedness, and they banished the murderer from their country forever.

The daughter of *Krakus* became the ruler of the country. Her name was *Wanda*, and she was very beautiful and, although she was but a young girl when she became Queen, she had wisdom and understanding far beyond her years. She loved her country very dearly and she ruled wisely and justly over the people who looked upon her with the greatest love and respect.

With all her qualities of beauty and wisdom, many princes sought her hand, but *Wanda* would accept none of them, for she had not yet found one who was pleasing in her sight and who would help her to rule wisely and well over her beloved country. Poland was dear to *Wanda*, and above all, she spared no effort to make the people happy. She waged war against aggressors who tried to invade her country, herself leading her soldiers in the battlefield. Her presence on the battlefield inspired the soldiers to defeat many foes.

Wanda's fame spread far and wide, and even a German Prince, named Rytigier, heard of her beauty, of her valor and, what was even more attractive to him, he heard that the lands of Poland were fruitful and rich. Prince Rytigier sent his emissaries with a letter to Wanda. The emissaries were received at Wanda's court with courtesy and typical Polish hospitality, as was always the custom in Poland. It was noticed that they were rough, uncivilized men who seemed surprised at the luxury and comfort of Wanda's Court. When the emissaries rested and changed their apparel, they were escorted into Wanda's presence. They made their bow before her, with seeming respect, they looked about them with an air of appraising the value of everything which they saw before them, as though it would soon be theirs.

Wanda read the letter which the emissaries brought to her and turned deathly pale. The contents were clear enough and the letter was an ultimatum for surrender to Prince Rytigier. The Prince asked for her hand in marriage, stipulating that as her dowry she should bring him the lands of Poland, and threat-

Princess Wanda Leaps into the Vistula River

ening waging a war on Poland in the event of a re-
fusal. Rytigier had a very strong army, famed all over
Europe, considered the strongest and best equipped
of any prince. Wanda's army, on the other hand, had
lost heavily in recent wars. To accept Rytigier's pro-
posal of marriage was tantamount to surrender and en-
slavement of the Polish nation. Wanda could not, and
would not subject her country to German rule. She
looked at the two emissaries and shuddered. Cruelty
and rapacity were written plainly in their faces. They
were typical Germans. To wage war might be fatal
with the armies so unevenly matched. Defeat at the
hands of the Germans would certainly bring the most
cruel reprisals to the Poles.

Queen Wanda was not scared and in a firm voice
made her answer known to the emissaries.

"I love my country and I love my people," said
Wanda. "I cannot sell them. To accept the offer of
Prince Rytigier would be equivalent to surrendering
myself and my country to the Germans."

The emissaries looked at Wanda with dismay and
returned to their country.

Wanda had made her decision. She would sacri-
fice her life for Poland.

She retired to her own apartments and prayed to
the gods that they would grant Poland freedom from
the Germans in return for her sacrificing her life. Her

prayer was granted, and Wanda threw herself into the Vistula River. When her body was recovered, she was buried with all honors, and a mound was raised to her memory beside that of her father, *Krakus*.

The story of *Wanda* is known in Poland, to every child, and her memory is respected and cherished as the brave Polish woman who died rather than give herself and her country to a German.

V. The Legend of the Piasts

MANY, MANY YEARS AGO, in the town of Gniezno (in old Slavonic language it means "nest") preparations were made for a great banquet. The occasion was the "shearing" of the two sons of the Prince. It was a pagan ritual, customary among the Slavs, for they were still pagans in those days. When a Slav boy reached the age of seven years, he had his hair shorn for the first time and had a name conferred upon him. The occasion was for great rejoicing and feasting. A large number of guests were invited. It was the custom for the most honored guest to perform the "shearing" ceremony.

Gniezno was bustling with great activity. It received many visitors from outside the city. The citizens, dressed in their best attire, thronged the streets. The gorgeously arrayed princes, riding their horses decked with ornamental saddles and adornments and followed by knights as gaily clad as themselves, came from neighboring states. They were greeted at the city gates with fanfares of trumpets. Then they rode through the city streets, greeted by an admiring crowd, and wound their way up the hill to the castle where the Prince received them, bowing low, and assuring them that all he possessed was theirs. Then he led his guests within the castle, and personally saw that they lacked nothing for their rest and refreshment.

Two travelers, weary, and dirty from travel, arrived at the gates of the city. They sought admission, but the guards stopped them and would not let them through. They asked the wanderers if they had been invited to the banquet which the Prince was giving for his sons, and on hearing that they had not, were abused and accused of being thieves. The two travelers protested their innocence and begged to be allowed to rest within the city. But the guards were adamant and turned them away. The people too, were angered, and started to throw stones at the unknown travelers who sought to enter their city. The two wanderers turned away, sad, disappointed and weary.

They walked away from *Gniezno* and, since God had directed their steps, they came to a humble and small cottage. It was built of mud-bricks, covered with thatch of straw and was surrounded by a modest garden in which grew some vegetables. In front of this cottage stood a man, poorly dressed, but with a strong and healthy look. He appeared to be in his early forties and was well built with broad shoulders. His hair and beard were fair. Beside him stood a boy of some

The Two Wanderers Meet the Piast

seven years, a fearless youngster, whose golden hair
fell in curls to his shoulders and whose blue eyes stared
at the strangers.

The man, noticing the weariness of the two travelers, approached them. His manner was direct, simple
and dignified. He asked them if they would rest within
his cottage, assuring them that they were welcome,
though the cottage was small and poor. They accepted
the gracious offer most willingly and, upon entering
the cottage, said: "Rejoice truly that we have come!
May you gain plenty, and honor and glory for your
progeny!"

It turned out that the owner of the cottage was a
ploughman to the Prince, and his name was *Piast*.
His wife's name was *Rzepicha*, which means "Little
Turnip." This does not indicate that she was common
or ugly. It meant that she was healthy and good, because men in those days lived chiefly on bread and
turnips, which were considered as a wholesome food.
Among the country people of Poland, even at the present time, an expression is made "healthy like a turnip."
Her name was rather a compliment to *Piast's* wife,
and she well deserved it. She was tall, beautifully built
and strong. The cottage was kept spotless, and the
earth floor was as clean as the floors in the Prince's
castle, if not cleaner. She baked the best bread of any
woman for miles around, and she was pleasant. Piast

was considered a fortunate man to have such a wife. She hastened forward to welcome her unknown guests, apologizing for the modest cottage and the lack of fine foods for them. She brought them milk and the freshly baked bread and instructed her son to serve them. They satisfied their hunger and thirst, and carried on a conversation with the hospitable *Piast* and *Rzepicha*. The couple were very much enlightened on many subjects and showed so much wisdom that the travelers knew they had found the man they were looking for. They resolved to carry out the mission which they had been sent to perform, and which was known only to them.

They asked *Piast* if he could give them anything to drink other than milk, and he replied:

"Indeed, I have a keg of fermented beer, which I have been keeping for the "shearing" of my son; it is the only one I have. But so what! Drink it, if you will."

Piast resolved to celebrate the "shearing" of his son at the same time as the Prince, for he was a poor man and he depended on the largesse, which his master would distribute among his people on this occasion, to provide for this. He intended to invite a few of his friends, not to a banquet, but to a simple supper. He had fattened the pig to regale his friends.

The travelers told *Piast* to pour out the beer, because they knew that it would not decrease in quantity by their drinking it, but rather increase. It did so, and became so abundant that it filled all the vessels which Rzepicha could borrow, and it was of such a rich quality as is only served at a Prince's banquet. The meat of the piglet was cut up, and it filled ten dishes and was so succulent, that none had ever tasted the like of it. *Piast* and *Rzepicha*, seeing this miracle, thought that it must foretell something very extraordinary for their son. They wished to invite the Prince and his companions to the "shearing" ritual, but they dared not until their guests advised them strongly to do so. The Prince and his companions were invited by the ploughman *Piast*. And the Prince did not think that he was conferring a great honor upon his ploughman by sitting at his table. In those days, Princes were not so great, nor had they pride and arrogance as they had in later times, and they were not surrounded by courtiers.

Piast and *Rzepicha* prepared a great banquet. Their little house was cleaned and scrubbed, bread was baked and the piglet's meat cooked. It was a great occasion for the good couple. *Rzepicha* was proud when the Prince praised her bread and her home and expressed pleasure at the good looks of her son. He himself, as the most honored guest, performed the ceremony of shearing the boy's head. *Rzepicha* wept when her boy's golden curls were shorn. What mother would not? She had been proud of those curls, and had tenderly stroked them when the boy sat at her feet or on her knees. But she was happy too, that her son was now growing up to be a young man, for after the "shearing" the boy was no longer considered a child. His education began preparing him for the duties of a man. The son of *Piast* and *Rzepicha* was given the name *Ziemowit*, as an augury of his future fate.

After this ceremony, young *Ziemowit*, son of *Piast* and *Rzepicha*, grew in strength and progressed from day to day. He became a knight and was well known. When *Popiel* disappeared from the country, the son of the Piast who had been the hospitable host of angels, and whose cottage had received a Prince, was made ruler. He won great glory for himself and the boundaries of his kingdom spread further than ever before.

After him reigned *Leszek*, his son, who rivalled his father in exploits and bravery. After the death of *Leszek*, his son, *Ziemomysl* ruled. Thus was the dynasty of the *Piasts* established.

VI. The Legend of Mieszko

ZIEMOMYSL OF POLAND had a son, Mieszko, who became great and famous. He was the first Prince of Poland, known by a foreign name. The chroniclers of the times referred to him as *Dago*. His fame became greater when he christianized Poland.

Mieszko was born blind. What a terrible sorrow it was to his parents, especially so when he was a beautiful and intelligent child. He had clear, pale grey eyes, and no person could tell that they were sightless until, looking closely, one would notice the lack of life in them when the boy stared emptily before him. *Mieszko* could not run like other lads, nor play, so he would sit beside his mother and fondle the ears of his dog, while he listened to the stories which she narrated him. They were stories of the brave deeds of his father and grandfather, of how his ancestor, *Piast* the ploughman, had given shelter and hospitality to two angels, of how the wicked King *Popiel* and his Queen had been eaten by the mice, and of how *Gniezno* was built. *Mieszko* was never tired of these tales, and begged to be told them over and over again.

When Mieszko's seventh birthday approached, his father called together all his councillors and dignitaries of the state to consult them regarding the banquet which should, according to custom, take place in honor of his son. *Ziemomysl* was not happy to have such a ceremony for his blind boy, because he was ashamed and he grieved that his son was afflicted. The councillors prevailed upon him, and the ceremony was arranged.

Mieszko was excited about the banquet, because it would be a change for him. There would be music, and he loved music. He would hear the laughter and merriment of the guests, and he would be allowed to taste mead, for his father had promised him this. The boy looked forward to this great day.

When the time came to dress him for the banquet, his old nurse found him high-spirited. He told her that he was sure that something wonderful will happen to him. The boy entered the great hall of the castle, led by the hand of his mother. He was dressed in a tunic of white velvet and his hose was laced up with gold. A golden circlet was on his brow. The young lad was led to a chair, where he sat in perfect silence, listening to the music. *Ziemomysl* watched him for a while, with a feeling of sadness.

There was dancing. The music of the flutes and cymbals was joyous and sweet. The dancers, moving gracefully, made an ever-changing pattern of bright colors. Suddenly, one of the ladies noticed that Mieszko was standing up, staring at the dancers with an expression of great delight. She left the dancing partner and walked up to him. The boy looked at her with a joyous smile.

"I can see," he whispered.

Mieszko's mother came hurrying up, for her mother's instinct had told her that something was happening to her son. At a glance she realized the truth, and threw her arms around Mieszko, clasping him to her breast. Some of the courtiers ran to tell Ziemomysl. They found him alone, sitting with his head in his hands, thinking of his boy.

"Sir," they told him, "your son can see."

Ziemomysl looked at them sharply. "What do you say?" he enquired of them. They repeated their assertion, but Ziemomysl would not believe them. He became angry because they annoyed him.

"Do not trifle with a father's feelings, the boy is blind and will always be so," he said angrily.

But then his wife came to him, laughing and crying at the same time, and threw herself on his breast.

"Mieszko can see, my dear," she said. "Come, I will show you."

And she led him by the hand to where the boy stood. Mieszko recognized his father and called him by name, as he did many other people, though he had not seen them before. Ziemomysl believed that his son was cured. Great was his joy, and great was the rejoicing of all those present. Dancing began all over with great vigor. The banquet was the occasion for drinking to the health of young Mieszko many times. Mieszko had his first draught of mead, after which he fell asleep and was put to bed.

This miraculous cure moved Ziemomysl and all his court. The Prince asked some old, wise men who were in the palace, what in their opinion, was the significance of this happening. Had it some special meaning? Was Mieszko destined to play a great part in the history of his country? The wise old men were puzzled, and pondered the questions profoundly, until one of them, older and wiser than the rest, gave the following explanation. The blindness which had afflicted Mieszko was symbolic of the blindness which afflicted Poland. Until his coming, Poland had been blind, but through Mieszko she would see, and be enlightened and raised above other nations. This explanation remained a mystery to Ziemomysl, who was never able to interpret it. But it really happened as the wise old man had foretold.

After regaining his sight, Mieszko began his education as a knight and as a prince. He grew up strong and fearless, he excelled in all manner of exercise,

Mieszko Takes Dombrowka for His Wife

and he was gentle and wise. He had understanding and intuition which ordinarily is rare among young men. This trait remained with him, perhaps, from the sad days of his blindness which he never forgot. He was a good and obedient son, and when his father died, he wept over his passing and buried him with the great honors.

Mieszko reigned in the place of his father, from the year 960, and he was a brave Prince. He fought many wars against aggressive neighbors who tried to invade Poland, and he defeated them all. He even threw them back and occupied their lands, and Poland grew into a strong, united country under his rule. Mieszko was still a pagan, and, according to pagan custom, he took unto himself seven wives.

When Mieszko met Dombrowka, a Czech princess and a good Christian, he fell in love with her. She was beautiful and good, and Mieszko wished to marry her. Dombrowka returned the love of Mieszko, but she refused to accept him unless he would renounce paganism and his seven wives and become a Christian like herself. Mieszko hesitated for a while, but his love for Dombrowka overcame all other considerations, and he proclaimed his readiness to become a Christian. He renounced his seven wives and prepared himself to embrace his new religion. The Czech princess herself came to Poland, as the recognized Queen of Poland, but she came with a splendid retinue of bishops and priests, and refused to accept *Mieszko* as her true husband until he should be baptized. *Dombrowka* herself instructed him, and under her training, *Mieszko* slowly but surely learned the doctrines of the Christian faith, until at last he was ready to be received into the Catholic Church. His baptism took place with great ceremony, in that very hall in which, many years before, he had recovered his sight.

All Poland followed the example of the King, and embraced the Christian faith, through the influence of *Dombrowka*. Thus were fulfilled the predictions of the wise old man, who said that Mieszko's blindness was a symbol of the blindness of Poland, which until then had been living in the errors of paganism, but which, under the influence of Mieszko and his wife, saw the light of the true worship of God, and thus became a truly great and enlightened nation.

VII. *The Legend of Saint Adalbert*

TOWARDS THE END of the tenth century, the Bishop of Prague, Adalbert, was invited by King *Boleslaw* of Poland to convert the Prussians, who were a pagan tribe living north of Poland. Bishop Adalbert set out with a few monks to preach the gospel of Jesus Christ to the Prussians.

As he approached the first Prussian settlement, he noticed a small cottage standing among the trees, quite alone. There was a large cluster of huts, some distance away. Adalbert was about to enquire of his monks if they knew to whom it belonged, when the owner, a poor widow, came forth and offered the Bishop rest and refreshment within her humble dwelling. The Bishop declined, however, saying that he must go on, for it was growing late. He accepted a cup of milk from the woman and gave her his blessing. He asked her if she was not afraid to live so near the settlement of a wild and pagan tribe, but she replied that she was so poor that they did not bother her. She added that the Prussians are greedy people

Bishop Adalbert on His Journey

and she begged the Bishop that he ought to be careful with them.

The little party continued on their journey, and soon reached the edge of the Prussian settlement. The tribesmen came out, heavily armed, and stared at the travelers, making threatening gestures and shouting. The Bishop, undaunted, held up his cross, which was inlaid with precious stones. This did not have the effect on the Prussians which he had hoped. Instead of being filled with reverence for the symbol of Christianity, the Prussians saw in it an object of value and they became greatly excited. They crowded around the Bishop, and eagerly stretched forth their hands. Adalbert ordered them back in a firm voice, at the same time putting the cross back in his bosom. This seemed to anger the Prussians and they pressed closer, seeking to tear the cross from Adalbert's neck, round which it hung on a golden chain. The Bishop, in his effort to keep his cross from irreverent pagan hands, was badly manhandled, and all the efforts of the monks to protect him were in vain. The Prussians became really angry, and one, bolder than the rest, lifted his club and struck Adalbert down. The other pagans fell upon him, and in a few moments the Bishop had breathed his last. The monks fled in terror and returned to Gniezno, where they informed Boleslaw of what had happened.

The Polish King was filled with anger and dismay. He shuddered to think what would happen to the body of Adalbert if it was with the pagan Prussians, and it was essential that the Bishop should receive Christian burial. He sent ambassadors to the Prussians at once, to demand the return of Adalbert's body. The ambassadors rushed out on their journey, reaching the same spot where Adalbert had been put to death. The Prussians who watched their arrival with some curiosity, now came forward, and, with some civility, enquired their will. The ambassadors demanded the body of Adalbert, Bishop of Prague, in the name of King *Boleslaw* of Poland. But the Prussians were not ready to part with their victim easily. They demanded the weight of the Bishop's body in gold, saying that otherwise they would not give it up. The ambassadors had some gold, though in no great quantity, but they trusted in God to save the body of His servant from desecration.

Two large baskets were brought and placed each at one end of a long plank which lay athwart a log. Into one basket was bundled the body of Adalbert, into the other, the gold which the envoys had brought. The weight of the body was far greater and the basket remained on the ground. The ambassadors took off their jewels, chains, rings, ornaments, threw them all into the basket, but still there was not enough. Then,

Emperor Otto Visits Gniezno

when all hope seemed lost, a poorly-clad woman approached. It was the same widow who gave the Bishop a cup of milk as he had journeyed towards the Prussians. She came forward holding in her hand a tiny gold coin. It was the only treasure which the poor woman possessed and had been part of her dowry, the only part which remained to her. She placed it in the basket, very shyly, as though ashamed of her humble offering. The Prussians began to laugh. Their laughter changed to amazement when the basket containing the gold began to sink slowly down until it reached the level of that containing the Bishop's body, then it stayed quite still; the balance was exact. The Prussians became surprised, a little afraid, and were deeply impressed. They soon became convinced that they were not all powerful, as they had thought, and became converted.

But this is not the end of the story. The Emperor Otto III, who was a Christian, wished to visit the tomb of Bishop St. Adalbert, because he was canonized. In the year 1000 A.D. there was a great Congress at Gniezno, and King Boleslaw solemnly received the Emperor. That same Otto III had received *Boleslaw's* father, Duke Mieszko I, as a vassal. But in Gniezno, as we mention elsewhere, he was received as an equal, and he did not hesitate to place his crown upon the head of *Boleslaw*, and to present him with the lance of St. Maurice. A chronicler tells us that Gniezno in those days was a magnificent city and that silver and gold were common there, as baser metals in other countries. *Boleslaw* was the first crowned King of Poland and he made her a great country.

VIII. Emperor Otto III Visits Gniezno

IT IS A KNOWN FACT that Emperor Otto III visited Gniezno in the year 1000 A.D. There is no actual contemporary written record of the visit, but the story was handed down from father to son, and here it is for the reader to enjoy.

Boleslaw the Brave was not yet King at the time. In the year 1000 he was still called Duke, but he was a powerful prince. In the capital of *Gniezno* were laid the remains of Saint Adalbert, or *Wojciech* as he is called in Poland. In his life Adalbert was a saintly man, who lost his life at the hands of the pagan Prussians.

It so happened that, not long after *Wojciech's* death, the year 1000 was born. A thousand years had passed since the birth of Christ. Men feared that the year 1000 would see the end of the world, and the Judgment Day. Many feared because they sinned. Pilgrimages were made to holy shrines, prayers were offered up, churches and monasteries were built and endowed, all in the hope that sins would be forgiven —if the world ended.

Otto III, Emperor of Germany and of the Holy Roman Empire, who had known Bishop Adalbert before his death, decided to make a pilgrimage to Gniezno, not only to pray for forgiveness at the tomb of the saint, but also to ascertain what manner of man was Duke *Boleslaw*. He heard much of the Polish ruler, of his power, of his skill and daring as a warrior, of his wise rule. Otto was a young man, he was only twenty years of age, but he had been Emperor since his earliest childhood and he, like all men at the time, had matured young so that he was a man of experience, despite his youth.

When *Boleslaw* heard of Otto's intention to visit *Gniezno*, he resolved to receive him in a most fitting manner. Otto was the most powerful prince in Europe. *Boleslaw* wished to show his mighty neighbor that Poland was a great country and worthy of the alliance with Germany.

As soon as the Emperor Otto reached the boundary line of Poland, he was met by a large number of church dignitaries, all dressed in ceremonial robes, and by many knights. These knights were mounted on powerful horses, and the excellence of their arms, the rich adornments of their horses, and the multitude and diversity of their banners, filled the Emperor and his retinue with astonishment. They had heard of the fighting valor of the Poles, but they expected to see

Emperor Otto Meets the Princes

fierce, wild warriors, armed with the most primitive weapons and probably dressed in skins. And here were knights, with courtly bearing and polished manners, mounted and armed as well as those in the service of the Emperor.

The knights guided the Emperor and his retinue through the lands which were unknown to them. A part of the country was wild and unpopulated, but those parts which were inhabited struck the visitors with their order and prosperity. The houses were well built of wood, the fields were tilled and the beasts were tended and the people looked happy and peaceful. Emperor Otto, a pious man, was well pleased to see that every village had its church, and in one of the larger villages, he expressed a wish to enter the church and pray. He dismounted accordingly and entered the wooden church. He was amazed with the beauty of the simple place of worship. The floor was strewn with rushes, on the walls were rough but colorful pictures representing the scenes from the Life of Christ, the lamps were bright, and flowers adorned the altar. The hands of pious and peace loving people had swept and garnished, and made the little church a bright and beautiful place. Emperor Otto began to feel respect as well as wonder for Poland.

The retinue proceeded on their way, they were joined by more and more knights with their mounted and armed attendants. They were well mounted, heavily armed, and richly attired. The Emperor thought that *Boleslaw* must indeed have a splendid army, that he must be a useful ally but a dangerous foe.

When they were near *Gniezno*, messengers spurred on to advise the Duke of the Emperor's arrival. *Boleslaw* rode out of his capital to greet his powerful and illustrious guest. And behind him rode a retinue of knights larger and more splendid than that which had accompanied Otto.

The two princes exchanged their greetings in solemn ceremony, each observing the other closely. *Boleslaw*, several years older than Otto, was taller and heavier built. There was a moment's silence, then Boleslaw spoke a few words of greeting and complimented his guest. Otto was astounded by the cordial greeting. The Polish Duke spoke in Latin. The German Emperor was very educated, for his tutor had been Gerbert, the French Bishop who afterwards became Pope Sylvester II, and who was one of the best educated men of his day. *Boleslaw*, who was famed as a warrior, had not neglected his education, and he was well able to converse with his guest.

They arrived at the gates of *Gniezno*. The capital was situated on a hill, and surrounded by strong wooden walls. At the gate, a great crowd had assembled to greet the guest. Otto dismounted, saying that he wished to continue the rest of the pilgrimage on foot. Hearing this, *Boleslaw,* also dismounted from his horse, ordered that red cloth should be laid in the streets through which the pilgrim should walk. After he had rested a short time, and refreshed himself with a draught of cooling wine, the Emperor set out on the last stage of his pilgrimage to the grave of the holy St. Adalbert (*Wojciech*). Reverently, with clasped hands, Emperor Otto walked through the streets of the capital of Poland as the silent, respectful crowds lined the streets, dressed in their finest attire. The Emperor noticed out of the corner of his eye, that the people in Poland were more prosperous than any townsmen that he had seen before.

When finally he came to the tomb of the Saint, he fell on his knees, and prayed long and fervently. The tomb, which was made of silver, richly adorned with precious stones and beautifully chased, shone in the light of a thousand candles.

When Otto completed his prayers, *Boleslaw* invited him to his castle, which was large, strongly built of wood and had enormous rooms, many turrets, guard rooms and all the offices typical of a princely residence.

Otto was escorted to his apartments, the furnishings of which were of surpassing richness. In a room adjoining that in which he was to sleep, was a huge basin made of silver, large enough for a man to step into. Attendants were filling it with warm water, richly perfumed. After he had bathed and changed his clothes, Otto was led to the banquet hall. This was a long, high ceiling chamber, with a raftered ceiling. The walls were covered with arms and weapons of all kinds, coats of mail, richly wrought helmets, lances, spears and swords. Long oak tables and benches were placed in the center and upon these were placed goblets and dishes of silver and gold. A great banquet followed. *Boleslaw*, dressed in great splendor, glittering with jewels, did the honors with all the grace and charm for which the warrior prince was famous in his own country.

The meats were cooked, spiced, and fried in honey. Game of every conceivable kind, fish cooked in wonderful sauces, sweets, spiced cakes, fruit, wines, mead and other most delicious and refreshing drinks were served. The eyes of the Germans opened wide, and they were impressed with what they saw. The German guests expressed their delight and enjoyment. They did full justice to the fare, and the Polish knights looked, in their turn, surprised and a little amused at such undisguised enjoyment of good food.

When the appetites were fully satisfied, conversation began. There were some interpreters, who were called upon to help, but with the Emperor and Boleslaw, these were not necessary. They carried on their conversation with ease in Latin. Otto asked many questions about Poland, which *Boleslaw* gladly answered. He told Otto about his army, about the produce of his country and about her riches.

Boleslaw ordered the servants to strip the walls of the banquet hall of all the rich weapons, and to gather together the gold and silver goblets and dishes, and to lay them at the feet of the Emperor whom he begged to accept this humble present.

The next day, a solemn High Mass was offered in the church at Gniezno, attended by both princes. This was celebrated with great splendor, and fervent prayers were offered up for the illustrious guest who came to the grave of the patron saint of Poland. After the Mass, there was another banquet, and to the Emperor's great surprise, the banquet hall, which had been stripped, was once again adorned with rich arms and the tables were covered with silver and gold. And at the end of the banquet, at which the fare was as splendid as ever, *Boleslaw* once again gave Otto all the arms and jewelled plates as a present.

The Emperor noted that here was a neighbor whom it would be worth while to have as a friend. He wished in some way to repay the kindness and hospitality of his host, and in a way befitting to an Emperor. He raised *Gniezno* to the dignity of an Archbishopric so that the Polish clergy would no longer be subject to the German clergy.

And Otto took the crown from his head, and placed it upon the head of *Boleslaw* saying: "Thou shalt be king." And thereafter *Boleslaw* was King of Poland, and was always known as King, though his solemn coronation took place twenty-five years later.

IX. The Legend of King Boleslaw and His Knights

WHEN KING BOLESLAW died, Poland lost a very able and brave ruler, one who had united her and made her into a really great country. Is *Boleslaw* lost to Poland? Some say no, for there is a legend about *Boleslaw* and his Knights, which I will tell you.

They say that *Boleslaw*, and his Knights who fought with him, went into a mountain called Giewont. He was a great warrior and earned the title of The Brave by routing Poland's enemies. The mountain of *Giewont* forms part of the Tatra, and its shape, as seen from a certain angle, is like the head of a sleeping knight. Within this mountain is a huge, dark cave and there sleep King *Boleslaw* the Brave and hundreds of his knights. They are mounted on their horses, with their swords beside them and lances couched. And if Poland needs them, then someone must awake them, and they will ride forth to serve her. But once they have gone forth, they will never return.

The legend tells us that hundreds of years ago a

blacksmith went every year to the cave to shoe the warrior's horses. This task had to be carried out in complete silence lest the warriors should awake and thinking that the summons had come, ride forth. The blacksmith who performed the task received a gold piece which was silently handed to him by the King himself, who sat silently on his horse near the entrance of the cave. No one knew whether the King slept or was awake, for his movements were so smooth, so deliberate, that he looked as a man in a trance. He always acknowledged the thanks of the blacksmith with a courtly inclination of the head, but none had ever beheld his eyes.

The task of shoeing the knight's horses had been handed down through the same family of blacksmiths from father to son for many, many generations. It was a much prized assignment and required unusual skill on account of the silence in which it had to be carried out. The danger of awakening the knights was impressed upon all those blacksmiths who undertook the assignment.

The shoeing was always performed at the same time of the year, in the spring. One year, the old blacksmith who had performed it for thirty years became ill, and he was unable to leave his bed. He was very much distressed at this, but his son, a strong young man who had been helping his father in the forge shop since he was a boy, assured him that he would carry out the assignment perfectly well.

"I shall have to do it one day," he said, "so why not today? Be assured, Father, that I will not speak a word to anyone about this."

The old man, still unconvinced, and muttering about the irresponsibility of youth, tried to leave his bed, but the pain was too great for him to rise, and he was forced to lie down again, and reluctantly allowed his son to go, with many parting warnings.

The young blacksmith started merrily off with his new horseshoes and his tools. His father gave him instructions where to light the fire with which to heat the shoes, and the order in which the knight's horses were shod, finishing with the King who was at the head of the array and nearest the entrance. When the young man arrived at the entrance to the cave, he felt a little nervous at the darkness, but he soon overcame this and looked eagerly around him. There, motionless, clad in rich armour and armed with swords, battle-axes and lances, sat the knights astride of their chargers. They were big men, for the most part, with clear-cut features and fair hair. At their head was King *Boleslaw*, with his long hair and fierce, curled moustache. Their horses were heavy, powerful beasts, some covered in armour, some with only a breast-plate and frontal piece, but all richly caparisoned. The young

The Knights of King Boleslaus

blacksmith, lost in contemplation, was forgetting his assignment, the shoeing of so many horses with their sleeping riders motionless astride them. The fire threw strange shadows on the walls of the cave, making the knights' shadows dance and assume gigantic proportions. The young blacksmith had almost completed his assignment, and when he was shoeing the last horse, that of the King, he dropped a red hot horseshoe on his foot.

"*Psiakrew!*" he cried, and, as he said it, the knights awoke.

"What? What?" he heard on every side.

"Did you call us? Answer, and we will come."

But he answered not and remained completely silent. The knights, after some more muttering, went back to their sleep. But as the blacksmith, after silently completing the shoeing of the King's horse, turned to go, he received a very sharp blow on the shoulders accompanied by a painful prod lower down.

King *Boleslaw* did not go back to sleep, and instead of a gold piece which the father usually received when he completed his assignment, the young blacksmith was given a sound drubbing. The young man fled. But since that day, no one has ventured into the cave, and the knights, with King *Boleslaw*, sleep undisturbed, waiting, waiting until they are called to fight for Poland for the last time.

X. The "Resurrected Brothers"

KING BOLESLAW the Brave was a great warrior, and he gathered around him many fearless knights who followed him to war against Poland's enemies. These knights were brave men, hot-blooded and daring, and their deeds in war were famous throughout Poland. In times of peace, however, some of the knights were not content with the chase, or with the tourneys, to give vent to their high spirits, and sometimes, though it was only very seldom, they would ride forth and attack parties of travelers and merchants, rob them and even, on occasion, kill them.

This was quite a usual occurrence in Germany, where the powerful were always anxious to increase their riches by robbing the weak. But in Poland such a practice was looked upon with disgust, and when reports of the knights' behavior reached King *Boleslaw*, he was very angry. He preserved justice in his country, and he made the weak feel as secure as the strong. He wished his country to be safe for travelers, hospitable for strangers. He had made good roads in Poland, wishing to encourage merchants from abroad to come into the country, bringing the goods which were so necessary to her. Was Poland's prosperity, her peacefulness, her very good name to be injured by a few hot-headed, high-spirited knights?

King *Boleslaw* was very angry, and he issued a decree whereby he proclaimed a death penalty for anyone who robbed or harmed a traveler. He was satisfied that this measure would put an end to such wicked ways.

But there were two young knights, brothers.

These two young men, not yet twenty, rode forth one day on a hunting expedition. They set out in great good spirits, hoping for a fine day's sport. But there was no sport. The beasts either took off to another part of the forest, or the wind was adverse to good hunting. They were disappointed as they rode home, their young faces sullen, their smooth brows furrowed with frowns. As they reached the road, they noticed a small band of travelers approaching. There were some elderly men on small horses, a large wagon drawn by oxen and driven by a stout-looking lad, and behind this, two heavily-laden camels, ridden by dusky, turbaned boys.

Eastern merchants! They were on the way to the capital of Poland with rich merchandise, lovely silks, woven in fantastic colors and gorgeous patterns, precious spices and fine-wrought jewels. The King would be pleased with this and would give much gold in return. The two brothers scowled at the little cavalcade. The younger, who was more hot-headed than his brother, said: "Here is sport for us, my brother. Come, let us attack them!"

Not heeding the King's decree, thinking not of the punishment, the knights rode at the party with all the speed they could muster, shouting ferociously. They scattered the frightened horsemen, pushed the lad off the cart, caused the camels to kick out and dislodge their riders, and created much confusion. The two brothers took very little booty after this, only a few jewels which, they thought, would please certain fair maidens.

The scattered merchants reassembled. They assisted the lad to his feet, and found that he was bruised and shaken. With difficulty the camels were quieted, their loads readjusted, their riders soothed. The merchants were very surprised at what had happened, for they had heard that the roads of Poland were safe from robbers.

When the merchants arrived in Gniezno, they were led before the King. Boleslaw questioned them closely on their journey, expressing the hope that they found the roads good and safe. The merchants told their story. They had been attacked by two young knights,

The "Resurrected Brothers" Released from
the Monastery

and robbed, though of very little, and one of their travelers had been hurt. King Boleslaw's brow grew black. He enquired where this had taken place, and ordered some of his guard to go there at once and to apprehend the two young knights.

The two offenders were feeling a little ashamed of themselves. Their hot temper had passed, and, being at heart brave men and true knights, they were very sorry for what they had done. When the guards came to take them to the King, their spirits sank and they became afraid. Now they recalled the King's decree and his anger against robbers. They were devoted to their sovereign, and would willingly have given their lives in his service, but they had been careless, as youth so often is.

They arrived at the King's court at *Gniezno* and stood before *Boleslaw*. His countenance was terrible to behold. He addressed the two offenders: "You, felons, criminals, you have broken the law, you have robbed peaceful, unarmed merchants, you have hurt a defenseless lad. You are not worthy to live in our good realm of Poland. You shall pay for this crime with your heads. You shall die."

All who heard the King's words were distressed, and grieved to see two strong and brave young men go to their death. But none dared to protest, for the King was a terror when he became angry. The two young knights did not dare to ask for pardon. They knew that they would not obtain it. They resigned to their fate and were led away in silence.

A few years passed.

Boleslaw was once again preparing for war against Poland's enemies. He summoned all his knights for the coming battle, and they came to Gniezno with great joy, willingly, and glad to give their services to Poland and their King. Boleslaw looked at them, greeting each one in his turn as an old friend.

That evening a great banquet took place which was attended by the Queen. The knights were happy, recalling former campaigns and former comrades-in-arms.

Some one mentioned the young brothers, saying that it was a pity that such brave, strong lads should have thrown away their lives for a foolish prank.

Noticing that her husband seemed to share this regret, the Queen said to him: "Dost thou not regret these two young knights, my husband? Wouldst you not be happy to see them alive once more?"

The King admitted that he would, that he would gladly set his eyes upon them once more and let them fight for their country.

The Queen fell at her husband's feet.

"Unbeknown to thee, my Lord, I saved the lives of those two brothers. I caused them to be sent to a monastery, where they are expiating their sins. Will thou forgive them? Will thou permit them to fight for Poland?"

King *Boleslaw* was happy to hear what the Queen had to tell him, and raising her, he embraced her saying: "Thou art a good and merciful woman. May God reward thee for thy virtuous heart."

Messengers were sent at once to the monastery in which the two brothers were confined, performing menial tasks for the monks and passing much of their time in prayer. When the two brothers heard the good news, they were filled with joy, and they returned to the King's court to throw themselves at the feet of the King and ask for forgiveness, and to thank the Queen, with all their hearts, for her intervention.

Everyone was happy to see them, and great was the rejoicing at court among the knights. The two brothers distinguished themselves in battle, and became Poland's two best known warriors, always given the name, because of their strange fortune, of "The Resurrected Brothers."

XI. The Trumpeter of Krakow

IN KRAKOW, the ancient capital of Poland, stands a church in the Market Square. It is a tall, graceful building of pink brick, built in the Gothic style, with richly adorned walls inside. The church has two towers, one of which is a little higher than the other and more ornate. From the taller tower a fanfare is played by a trumpeter, every hour. It is repeated four times, but it always ends abruptly, on a broken note.

This is the story of the "Hejnal," as it is called.

From the tower of St. Mary's Church, for centuries past, the *Hejnal*, or Hymn to Our Lady (whose Church it is), was played by a trumpeter. He played it four times—to the four winds—and he played it every hour. One day, many, many years ago, as he played, the trumpeter saw in the distance a cloud of dust which grew bigger with every passing moment. It was a large army of Tartars galloping towards the city. These cruel invaders from the east had more than once advanced to *Krakow*, even farther, and they had pillaged and burnt, looted and murdered and carried off the young people to be slaves in their camps. The trumpeter was horror-stricken. How could he warn the city, how could he convey to the people the approach of danger and give them time to prepare their defense? There was only one thing he could do. To go down into the town and spread the alarm would be foolish, for it would be impossible to cover the whole town in the few minutes. He decided to play the *Hejnal*, over and over until all the town people would awake and prepare for the invasion. That would surely rouse the citizens, they would be aware of the approaching danger. So he played, again and again.

At first the people of *Krakow* were puzzled. Why was the trumpeter playing over and over the same tune? And with such loud urgency? But the people quickly realized that it was a warning and that from his lofty tower he had seen danger approaching. The soldiers sprang to arms and took up their stations on the walls of the city. The burgesses ran to secure their homes and place their wives and children behind locked doors. The apprentices seized their arrows and their cross-bows, the artisans seized what tools they could lay hands on, and they all marched to the defense of their city. Suddenly, the sound of the Hejnal stopped abruptly. The notes had reached the ears of the Tartars as they approached, and their keen eyes spotted the figure of the trumpeter in the tower. As soon as they came within a bow-shot, their leader, the best marksman of them all, loosed his bow, and the deadly projectile lodged in the trumpeter's throat.

But his assignment was accomplished, and *Krakow* was saved. Thanks to his warning, the people were able to defend the city, and they inflicted a crushing defeat on the Tartars, killing one of their princes.

And since that day, the Hejnal has been broken off at the same note on which it was broken off by the Tartar arrow, in honor of the trumpeter who gave his life for the city.

That is the legend of the trumpeter of *Krakow*. Many historians, not being able to find written documents to prove the story, asserted that it was not true, and that it was just a popular tale. They said that the Tartars had never fallen unexpectedly on the city of *Krakow*, and, if they had been Tartars why, in the annual pageant held to commemorate the event, were the "invaders" dressed in clothes which resembled the people of far-eastern lands, than those of Crimea from where the Tartars came? But many people believe in legends, affirming that there is always some base for legends and that a story handed down for generations and known to a whole village or district, is more likely to be true than an account found on an ancient parchment in a dusty archive and written by the hand of one man alone.

The Trumpeter of Krakow

A Polish officer, a former student of *Krakow* University, was taken prisoner by the Russian army in 1939. After his release two years later he found himself, after some wandering, with others of the Polish army in Samarkand, the ancient capital of Tamerlane. Under its former name of Maracanda, the city had been destroyed by Alexander the Great, but centuries later, under Tamerlane, it had once again become a great and prosperous city. It has since declined, but the people, who are Muslims, recall their former greatness.

These people, living in a remote place, had heard little of Europe and its countries. But one country they knew: Lechistan—an ancient name given to a country which was later known as Poland.

They greeted their guests of the Polish army with traditional oriental courtesy. But when they heard that these guests were from Lechistan, they showed signs of keen interest.

"So you are truly the sons of Lechistan?" they asked.

"We are," replied the Polish soldiers.

"And you are the soldiers?"

"Yes."

Then, after a silence:

"You believe in God? The same God in which you believed long ago?"

"Yes, we do; we have priests; see, we wear crosses," and the soldiers drew forth small crosses from beneath their uniforms, crosses cut from a tin can, since there were no others.

The people of Samarkand looked upon these crosses with a strange joy. But the next question seemed strangely irrelevant.

"And you have trumpeters?"

"We have."

A silence, and then, shyly:

"We have a request to make. If you are from Lechistan, and you are soldiers, and you believe in your ancient God, and you have trumpeters, could you—could you ask those trumpeters to play tomorrow evening in the old market square? Opposite the Mosque where lie the ashes of Great Timur?"

The Polish soldiers agreed, puzzled, and they were still more puzzled by the large, silent crowd which had assembled in the square.

They played a reveille, they played regimental marches and at last they played the Hejnal. There was complete silence in the square, and in silence the people dispersed. It seemed that they were very happy, but they would not speak.

It was only a little later that the Poles learned the reason for the strange request, and for the joy of the people. There is, it seems, a legend too, in Samarkand. And this was the story they heard.

Once, long ago, the people of Samarkand took part with the Tatars in one of the invasions of Poland. And they came to a city which, they say, was the same for Lechistan as Samarkand was for them. It was a capital, a very old, very rich city. And it was a holy city, for from one of the minarets a trumpeter called the people to prayer. The Tartars wished to take the city by surprise, but the trumpeter was able to alarm the citizens before a Tartar arrow killed him, lodging in his throat. The city defended itself and the Tartars were defeated.

A Tatar prince was killed and the elders and priests, to whom a report of the faith was given, pronounced it was a punishment from Heaven, for killing a man who called the people to prayer. And they predicted that Samarkand would lose her greatness, would lose her liberty. The prosperity would return to Samarkand, though not until trumpeters from Lechistan should play in the market square that same song which was cut short by the arrow of the Tartar.

XII. The Legend of Lech, Czech and Rus

MORE THAN A THOUSAND years ago, there lived a king who ruled over the lands that lay near the mouth of the Danube River. When the king died, his wealth was left to the care of his three sons. When the three brothers became aware that their father's small domain was not large enough to be split between them, they were very unhappy. Each one wished to rule, yet all three could not rule upon the same throne, nor was there enough land to be divided among themselves.

Rather than fight among themselves, they decided to search for other lands which would be large enough to satisfy their needs. They started on their journey and found themselves in strange lands, meeting with many dangers and with wide assortment of wild animals, dangerous serpents and savage men.

While walking through the road, one of the brothers gazed upwards. He saw three eagles high in the air. At first he thought nothing of this because birds were a common sight, and there were a number of them flying in every direction and at various heights. What bothered him was the fact the birds were following along with them. This was considered unusual. The brothers were joking about the incident.

"I choose the white bird," said *Lech*, the eldest brother.

"And I choose the black one," said *Rus*.

"Then I must take the only one left," exclaimed *Czech*, and in this choice of birds they passed the time as they continued on their travels.

At last the three brothers came to three roads, diverging like the rays of a fan. One road led to the north, the direction in which they were originally destined to continue their journey. Another road was turned to the northeast, and the third road pointed to the northwest.

"Which road shall we take?" asked one of them as they halted their footsteps in order to decide the important question.

"I am all set to go straight on," *Lech* said.

"And I too was heading in the same direction," said the others. "There is no reason why we should separate so soon. Let us wait!"

As they argued the point back and forth, *Lech* saw the white eagle, the one he had chosen, winging its way to the north, and the two remaining birds each followed the direction of the other two diverging roads.

"There goes your bird," Lech said to his brother Rus, as he pointed to the black eagle flying to the right.

"Mine goes straight onward," continued Lech, "and so I shall also go. As for the rest of you, you may do what you please."

"Then I shall follow my bird," Rus replied. "Perhaps it may bring us all good luck."

The three brothers parted with affectionate farewells.

Rus followed the black eagle until he came to the country of Russia, which he founded and named after himself.

Czech came to the country of Bohemia, which in later years became known as Czecho-Slovakia because its inhabitants were Czechs.

And as for Lech (he went north until he came to the broad plain where he settled. Inasmuch as his guide was a white eagle, he decided to appropriate the bird and use it as an emblem. In this way, it happened that Poland has a white eagle upon its flag.

Lech settled in an immense plain, the Polish word for which is "Pola," and then Lech added his own name to that, making Po-Lech, sometimes written as Lach. In this way the "Po-Lachs" or as they called themselves "Polacks" came to be. They were the people of *Lech* who settled the plains.

The chroniclers tell us that the three brothers—*Lech, Czech* and *Rus* were waging a keen strife among themselves, and that they met at the *Warta* to make peace. There they found an island settled by fishing people. The place where *Lech* stayed he built a town, called *Poznan* because of this meeting (*Poznanie*).

So goes one more legend that tells us how Poland began, over a thousand years ago.

THE END

DATE DUE